Praise for

They Didn't Teach THIS in Worm School!

"Lia's understated visual humour goes
hand in hand with joyfully surreal adventures"
Guardian

"Laugh-out-loud and full of wonderfully
funny illustrations ... a must-read for
anyone with a sense of adventure"
Red Reading Hub

"Marcus and Laurence are hugely loveable
characters and this beautifully illustrated book
will carry you swiftly to its sweet conclusion"
Booktrust

"Sprinkled with funny illustrations and lots of laughs"
South Wales Evening Post

"A comedy classic that will have
readers wriggling with laughter"
WorldBookDay.com

"It's as hilarious as a chicken in a cat suit"
The Phoenix

"This is a gentle, touching story with many laugh out loud
moments and plenty of expressive pictures."

They didn't teach THIS in worm school!

They didn't teach THIS in worm school!

Simone Lia

WALKER
BOOKS

First published in Great Britain 2016 by Walker Books Ltd
87 Vauxhall Walk, London SE11 5HJ

This paperback edition published 2017

10 9 8 7 6 5 4 3 2 1

Printed and bound in China

British Library Cataloguing in Publication Data:
a catalogue record for this book is available from the British Library

ISBN 978-1-4063-7334-9

www.walker.co.uk

For Timothy

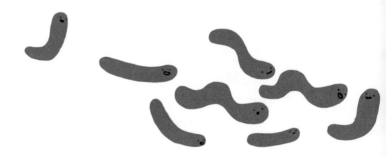

Chapter One

My name is Marcus.

I am a worm and this is where I live.

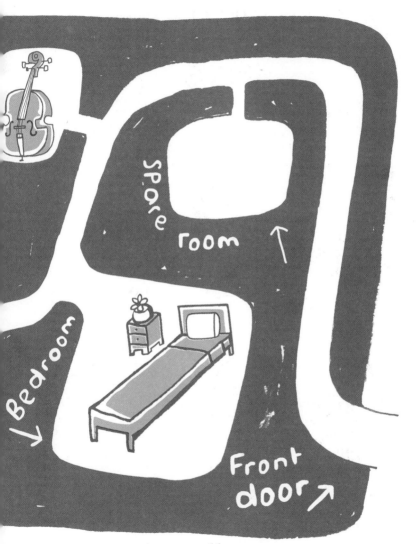

My favourite colour is brown.

That's because mud is brown and I really, really, really like mud.

My favourite things are other worms.

And my hobby is digging holes in the ground. There is nothing I enjoy more than making a complicated underground tunnel system.

But when I met Laurence, everything changed.

Let me tell you about how I met him...

I was digging a hole, like I usually do (like all worms do), but I must have fallen asleep because the next thing that happened was that I was flying a spaceship in outer space.

The spaceship was made out of potatoes.

Then, I dreamt I fell out of a can into a cereal bowl. Staring at me was a scruffy, fat bird who looked a lot like a chicken. It was a really good dream until it got to the bird part. The bird had intense and menacing eyes.

14

The worst thing was that the last part of the dream wasn't a dream at all. I really had been in a can and there really was a big, fat bird staring at me!

What would you do if you were a worm and there was a bird two centimetres away from your face looking at you with his beak open so wide that you could see his tonsils?

Maybe you would do what I did. I smiled a big smile and said in my most cheerful voice,

Good morning!

The bird looked confused. He mumbled "Good morning" back and then opened his beak again with his head tilted at a slightly different angle.

Before he could eat me up, I shouted very loudly and quickly, "MY NAME IS 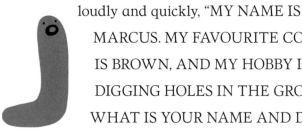 MARCUS. MY FAVOURITE COLOUR IS BROWN, AND MY HOBBY IS DIGGING HOLES IN THE GROUND. WHAT IS YOUR NAME AND DO YOU HAVE A HOBBY, PLEASE, SIR?"

I added a "sir" at the end to be polite.

The bird seemed taken aback. He closed his beak.

"My name is Laurence," he said.

He was about to open his beak again. "AND WHAT about hobbies?" I asked. "DO you have a nice HOBBY, Laurence?"

Laurence sat down, looked at his fat belly and then looked at me again. "No one's ever asked me that question before," he said.

"Really? WELL take your TIME and make yourself COMFORTABLE," I said, encouraging him to lie down on the sofa. I positioned myself a little bit closer to the window. "I'd love to hear all about your hobby. It is very, VERY interesting."

I didn't mean to keep shouting, but I was
scared and I didn't quite know what I was doing.
Laurence didn't seem to notice. He obediently
put his feet up.

"My hobby is travelling," he said.

"How fascinating!" I said, trying not to shout
as much. "And where have you been to?"

Laurence thought for a while. "That's the
problem," he explained. "I haven't been anywhere.
I'm terrible at map-reading. I'd love to visit Kenya
in Africa, but it's such a long way to fly, I would
definitely need a map to get there."

I paused to try to give the impression
that I was thinking deeply about what he

was saying.

"Why ... Kenya?"

While he was
thinking of his answer,
I looked out of the
window.

We were in
a birdhouse
in a tall tree.
The latch on
the window
was too high
for me to reach.
Even if I could
have reached
and pushed
the window
open, I wasn't
too keen on
wriggling down
the tree from
that height.
They didn't
teach us how
to do that at
worm school.

Laurence was looking at his belly again. Why did he keep looking at his stomach? Was it because it was large, or was it because he was hungry? I decided to keep talking to distract his mind from food thoughts. "Tell me what it is about Kenya that you love so much."

Laurence sat up. "I'll show you," he said, reaching for a glossy travel book from a pile of books on the floor. He opened it. "This is the Maasai Mara National Reserve. Look at these beautiful wide open plains. There are so many animals that live in the nature reserves in Kenya. You just don't see animals like that around here." Laurence flicked through pages with photographs of lions, elephants, zebras and wildebeest. He stopped at a page that had pictures of pink birds with skinny legs.

"*This*," he said, slamming his wing on the page dramatically, "is why I need to go." Laurence looked at me. "Do you see what I mean?"

"Hmm ... yes," I said, nodding in agreement, pretending to understand what he meant.

"Thank you. I'm glad that you see it too – that I am actually a flamingo."

"A flamingo," I repeated firmly, trying my best not to laugh out loud. Laurence doesn't look anything like a flamingo.

A FLAMINGO

He looks like a chicken.

LAURENCE

"I don't belong here with ordinary birds. I belong *here*," he paused to read the caption at the bottom of the photograph, "in the Lake Nakuru National Park, with other flamingos. That is my real home, and it is the only place where I can be truly happy." He slammed the book shut and clasped his wings together.

The thing that stopped me from laughing at Laurence was the fact that I was in a very bad situation. At any moment he would remember how hungry he was and slurp me up like a piece of spaghetti. I needed to use every part of my worm brain to come up with a cunning plan to escape from the birdhouse.

MY WORM BRAIN

Instead, I accidentally blurted out my
worst fear:

Are you going to eat me for breakfast?

"Probably not," said Laurence, sighing. "It feels
funny eating you for breakfast now that we've
had a conversation."

I almost felt relieved at this, but I was not
reassured by Laurence's use of the word probably.
Keeping the conversation going seemed like
a good idea.

"What's to stop you flying to that park in
Lake Nakuru?" I asked.

"I told you, I can't read a map. I don't know the way," said Laurence, standing up and facing the wall, unable to meet my eyes.

I wriggled on the floor to where he stood and said softly, "Laurence, you must follow your dreams. If Lake Nakuru is where you belong, then surely there will be a way for you to fly there... There will be a way."

It suddenly felt like we were in a film. It was
an excellent film.

If Laurence did fly to Kenya, then he wouldn't
be able to eat me for breakfast or lunch or dinner.
"There must be a way," I continued.

Laurence sighed, then looked at me with those
intense eyes. "Tell me about your hobby again,"
he said, beckoning me to sit on the sofa.

"Umm…" I was a bit worried about the look in his eyes but thought it might be best to keep talking. "I like digging holes in the mud. It's very relaxing, and I make escape tunnels to interesting places, like near a tree so that I can eat apples that have fallen on the ground, or near the compost heap, which is fun, it's a bit like going to the beach and—"

"Don't you get lost when you're underground?" asked Laurence, interrupting me. "It must be quite dark down there."

"No. I always know where I am. I just kind of feel it."

"That's THAT, then!" said Laurence, triumphantly laughing and clapping his wings together.

"What's WHAT?" I asked, feeling quite worried again.

"You, Marcus, with your funny ideas and marvellous sense of direction – you can help me fly to Kenya. You can be the navigator! And to think that I almost ate you for breakfast—"

I was shouting again.

We were going to fly to Lake Nakuru National Park.

I had no choice.

It was either that or be eaten for breakfast.

Chapter Two

Laurence was packing for the long journey ahead.
He was excited, singing and whistling as he
hurried around his birdhouse.

I sat on the sofa and looked out of the window.
It was a sunny day. I wished that I was outside.
Or at home, under the ground. Or anywhere

that wasn't here on
this sofa, waiting
to go somewhere I
didn't want to go
to, with someone
whom I didn't
want to go with.

There was no way for me to escape. I'd just have to fly to Lake Nakuru with Laurence and start a new life. I'd send Auntie and Uncle a postcard when I got there, so they would know where I was.

Dear Auntie and Uncle.
I live in kenya now. It's lovely weather here.
Love you!
marcus

1 worm st
WORMETON
WORMSHIRE
ENGLAND

"I'm just having a DUST BATH," shouted Laurence cheerfully from the bathroom. "I'll be ready SOON. We're going to have so much FUN!"

"YES," I said. I was really worried now. Not only did Laurence think that I could read a map, but he also seemed to think that I knew how to fly.

Had he not noticed that I don't have wings? What would he do when he found out that I can't do that, either?

Laurence was ready. He was carrying a big map and a small leather bag. "Here, you'll need this," he said, throwing the map towards me. "To work out the route."

I looked at Laurence's bag. A thought popped into my worm brain. "Have you got everything that you need in that very small and tiny bag?"

"I think so. I've got a reading book, a big sandwich and my blanket in case it gets cold at night."

"Oh..." I said.

"What do you mean 'oh'?" asked Laurence.

"Nothing. Well. It's just that ... it's a long way and you might get bored. I thought you might need some other things. You know, for entertainment."

"I see. Well, I could take my yo-yo."

"And would you need any of these travel books? What's this one?" I asked, flicking through the pages.

"Yes, I'd better bring that one – it's about Paris. That's the Eiffel Tower... We'll probably see that on the way."

"And what about the television set?"

"Do you think we'll need that?"

"Yes. They might not have TV at Lake Nakuru."

"Oh. I hadn't thought of that. In that case, I'd better take the computer as well. And

the printer."

"And you might need some warm clothes to wear."

"But I think it will be hot there."

"Well, you'll definitely need to take an electric fan, then...

"GOSH!" I exclaimed loudly.

"What?" asked Laurence, looking worried.

"Toilets!"

"What about toilets?"

"Will there be any on the way?"

"I don't know! I'd better take my own toilet," Laurence replied quickly.

"And what about eating? I mean SEATING?" I said, suddenly remembering to avoid food-related subjects.

Laurence looked at me and held his wing finger aloft.

"Do you mind waiting in here while I pack some more things, Marcus?"

"Not at all," I said. "Take your time."

Laurence went into his bedroom. I could hear him opening drawers and cupboards. It sounded like he was pushing furniture around. Then there were clanking noises coming from the bathroom as he disconnected the toilet from the pipes.

When he returned, he was carrying much
more than his little travel bag.

"Do you think that I'm going to be able
to fly like this, Marcus?"

I looked at him. "Probably not," I said,
shaking my head sadly. "It might be better
if you don't go..."

Laurence laughed. "Of course we're going to go. I probably don't need most of these things. I'll unpack again. Thanks for thinking of me, though," he said sincerely.

"No problem," I said, feeling a bit guilty.

After several hours of unpacking and re-connecting the plumbing works, we were ready to leave.

Laurence opened the front door.

"I DON'T KNOW HOW TO FLY, LAURENCE," I shouted up to him. "DO YOU MIND IF I STAY HERE?"

Laurence laughed again. "Silly, I know that worms can't fly!"

He bent his head down as an invitation for me to climb up onto the back of his neck.

I wriggled up.

"Is that comfortable?" he asked.

"YES!" I said, and I wasn't lying. I was surrounded by a million soft feathers. It was like sitting on a cloud in heaven.

We were ready to leave.

Chapter Three

"I'm going to jump from the platform now, Marcus, and then we're going to fly up through the tree. You might feel some leaves brushing past as we go. Are you ready for that?"

"OK! I'm ready," I said, closing my eyes.

"Hold tight!" he said.

I could feel Laurence take a hop and then a leap. Laurence flapped his wings noisily as we flew up into the tree. Twigs and leaves hit me in the face. I clenched every part of my worm body tightly. After what seemed like ages, I opened my eyes. We'd flown up into the sunny blue sky.

Just to remind you, in case you had forgotten, I am a worm. I usually spend my time in the dark, under the ground. But now I was sitting on this super-soft, flying bird cushion. Up high in the sky. When I looked down, I could see the trees and the houses below getting smaller and smaller. I felt so many things at once – amazed, excited and terrified. Part of me wanted to take a little nap and forget that this was happening. And another part of me wanted to be sick; my worm stomach felt really funny all of a sudden.

"Are you OK?" Laurence asked.

I couldn't speak. The wind was flapping against my face.

"If you feel a bit FUNNY, look at the HORIZON," Laurence shouted. "Please try not to be SICK ON ME."

I looked ahead at the green and brown fields. Looking at the view made my stomach forget that it was upset.

"When you're ready, Marcus, open up the map and tell me which way we need to fly. We need to head south towards France. See if you can FIND THE WAY TO PARIS."

"OK!" I shouted back. There were a lot of things to think about. I was almost getting the hang of this flying business. I unfolded the large map, suddenly feeling confident about my new job as a navigator.

Immediately, a gust of wind caught the map and tossed it into the air. I watched as it became a small square speck in the distance.

That's the end of my navigation career, I thought to myself. Without a map I was of no use to Laurence. What would he do when he found out? Would he eat me for his lunch? Or maybe he'd keep me for his dinner. There was not a lot I could do until he'd made a decision about when to eat me. *Until then, I may as well relax and enjoy the ride,* I thought, snuggling deeper into Laurence's soft feathers.

"We need to cross the English Channel first. Have you seen it on the map?" Laurence asked. "It's blue."

"Umm ... oh yes," I lied. "It's on the right."

Laurence turned his body and we flew towards some bright yellow fields. *That worked quite well,* I thought to myself.

I could see a horse in a far-off field, galloping in a paddock. "Fly towards the horse and then turn left," I said.

Laurence changed direction again. It was brilliant! Laurence was doing everything that I asked him to do. This was better than flying a potato in my potato spaceship dream.

"Fly higher!" We went up and up, until I could hardly breathe.

"Lower," I said, and we flew so low that
the grass swished against Laurence's fat belly.

"Now do a loop the loop."

weeeee!

That was a good one. Afterwards, I had to
concentrate on the horizon again.

Laurence didn't question any of my instructions until I said, "Now fly backwards."

"Does the map *really* say that?" Laurence called up to me.

Umm...

"I've got a funny feeling about this, Marcus. You *do* know how to map-read, don't you?"

I didn't say anything. I was a little bit worried that he might change his mind about eating me for breakfast if I told him the truth. Laurence turned around to look at me.

"You haven't even got the map!" He was angry now. "THAT'S IT."

When I'm sad or frightened, I quite like to burrow into the earth. It's very calming and relaxing being in the ground, surrounded by lovely, cool, safe mud. Forgetting where I was, I flopped over and dug into Laurence's soft feathery wing.

But digging a hole in the ground is not the same as digging a hole in the sky. I found this out the hard way.

One moment I was comfortably perched on Laurence's back, surrounded by a million soft feathers, and the next moment there was nothing there at all. It was just air. I spun and tumbled, free-falling speedily towards the broccoli-looking trees. I closed my eyes and tried to multiply 2,657 by 6,765 in my head.

I'm not sure if I did work out the answer
because the next thing I knew I was sleeping in
a very comfortable bed that felt as though it was
made out of mashed potatoes.

I opened my eyes. Laurence was looking at me.
There was no mashed potato bed. I was lying on
my back on the grass, in a field. "Where are the
mashed potatoes?" I asked Laurence sleepily.

"There are no mashed potatoes. You must have been dreaming. Are you OK?" he asked with a worried look on his face.

"I think so," I said, sitting up.

Laurence folded his wings across his front. The worried look went away and he was cross again. "You told me that you knew how to map-read."

"No, I didn't!" I'd said things to Laurence that weren't quite true, but I was sure that I hadn't said that I could map-read.

"You did."

"No, I didn't." I was beginning to get cross. "You're really mean, Laurence! I don't want to be here any more. I'm going home."

I got up from my bed of grass and wriggled further into the field. I wanted to get away from Laurence as fast as I could.

"Pbbt! You don't even know where you're going!" Laurence called out to me.

"Yes, I do," I said, lying again. I didn't know what to do. I was lost, but I couldn't turn back. I wriggled some way and stopped to think, pretending that I was admiring the view.

As I was pretending to admire the view, I noticed that there actually *was* a view. And it looked oddly familiar, just like the cover of Laurence's French guidebook...

Was it?

It *was*...

The Eiffel Tower!

"Laurence!" I said, forgetting that I was upset with him.

"What? Are you going to admit that you're lost?"

"I'm NOT lost. I know exactly where we are."

"No, you don't."

"I do! We're in Paris."

"No, we're not," he said, hopping over to stand next to me.

We both looked at the Eiffel Tower.

"Oh," he said with bright eyes and a smile on his beak. "So we are."

The sun was setting, casting a long shadow on this famous landmark.

It was spectacular.

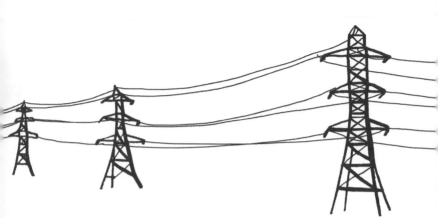

Chapter Four

We'd been looking at the Eiffel Tower for some time. It didn't look exactly like the picture in the book. The shape was similar, but there was something that seemed different. At the top there were tight wires that connected it to ... other Eiffel Towers. There were Eiffel Towers everywhere, as far as the eye could see.

Things must have changed since the photo in the book had been taken, I thought to myself.

"That's progress for you," I said out loud, by accident.

I wriggled my way over to the Eiffel Tower to get a closer look, and Laurence hopped after me. We stood beneath it, looking up.

"I must have taken us a special shortcut way. It didn't seem to take that long."

Laurence laughed without opening his beak. "Yes, it took no time at all. I don't even remember flying over the Channel."

"I think that we did. I saw some ducks," I replied, pleased that Laurence seemed to have forgotten about the map fiasco.

"Oh, I thought that was a pond," Laurence said. He opened up his little bag, which had been tucked into his feathers. He took out an itchy-looking blanket, shaking it roughly. The blanket must have reminded him of the map that I had lost, because he suddenly remembered that he was angry.

"I'm still upset with you," Laurence said. "You made me think that you were good at map-reading. It's only by luck that we ended up here in Paris. You're just as bad at directions as I am!"

He lay down on the ground and pulled the blanket over him so that it was tucked under his beak. "I wish that I'd stayed at home."

"Well," I said, lying down next to him. "I didn't even want to come. I'd much rather be at home." I pulled some of his blanket towards me and turned my back to him.

"Good night," I said crossly.

"Hmph. Good night," he replied, while taking the covers back to himself again.

We'd travelled a very long way. The sun had set, and the stars were shining through the blackened sky. I thought about a plan for the next day.

I'd get up early before Laurence woke and had time to think about what he might eat for breakfast. Then I'd have a wander around, looking at all of the

Eiffel Towers and seeing if there was anything else of interest in Paris. I'd send a postcard to everyone back home to let them know that I'd be living here now. Then I'd take some French lessons and begin my new life, here in France.

I began counting the stars. On the four-hundred-and-eighty-fourth star, I fell asleep.

Chapter Five

I slept heavily that night, under the stars. Early
the next morning, I stretched my worm body
and yawned a great big yawn. I opened my eyes,
expecting to see Laurence's grumpy face, an itchy
blanket and a row of Eiffel Towers in a field.

But there was no field.

And there were no Eiffel Towers, either. Laurence and I were not lying beneath an itchy blanket. We were both sitting on a leather sofa, and sitting next to us was a mole with long, sharp claws. He was gently stroking the arm of the sofa.

I looked at Laurence for some clues as to what might be happening. He had an expression on his face that I'd not seen before.

My worm instincts were telling me that something was not quite right.

The evil-looking French mole, Laurence and I were in some kind of a shelter. It was quite dark in there, but when my eyes adjusted to the dim and smoky light, I could see that the roof and walls were made from cardboard and plastic bottles.

The floor was bare soil.
A scrawny squirrel with
horrible teeth stood at the
opening of the shelter, staring
at me and cleaning her front
tooth with a twig. A creepy
crow was on the other side
of the door. He was using a
wooden spoon to stir the contents of a large

metal pot that was
balancing over
a fire.

"I'd like to go home now, please,"
I whispered to Laurence.

"You need to BE QUIET, Marcus.
Just try to ACT NORMAL,"
Laurence whispered back, very loudly.

The mole overheard our conversation. He
seemed to understand English. "*Relaaax, Marcus.
And you, chicken bird. We're making breakfast.
It's going to be a delicious stew.*" He spoke with
a perfect English accent.

"I DON'T LIKE STEW,"
Laurence blurted out.

"You'll like this one," said
the mole. "It's a *chicken* and
worm stew." He laughed,
and then the crow and
the squirrel laughed too.

Neither Laurence nor I laughed at his joke
because we both knew that he meant us (even
though Laurence isn't a chicken).

"I THINK THAT I NEED TO USE THE BATHROOM NOW," Laurence said loudly. Everyone stopped laughing. The crow dropped the spoon into the pot. He moved over to block the doorway. The squirrel stood behind him with her arms folded; she was chewing vigorously on her twig.

"You DON'T need to use the bathroom," said the mole, firmly. Everyone looked at Laurence.

Laurence thought for a moment.

"You're right," he said softly. "It was a FALSE ALARM."

No one said anything. Laurence was now gently rocking backwards and forwards on the seat, cradling his head with his wings. I daydreamed about being somewhere different. It would be quite good to be wandering around Paris right now.

64

ding ding

Perhaps riding a bicycle with
a wicker basket on the front
that held a freshly baked
baguette.

Then I remembered that I didn't know how to
ride a bicycle, and then I remembered where I was
and whom I was with.

Ever since I'd known Laurence, all that he had
ever brought me was trouble. First he almost ate
me for breakfast, and now, because he looked
like a chicken and I happened to be sitting next
to him, I was going to end up as lunch.

He was like an unlucky charm. I needed to
get away from him and as far away from that
cooking pot as possible. An idea floated into my
worm brain. I cleared my throat.

"Excuse me, Mr Mole. I was
thinking about your stew. Do
you mind if I give you a tip to
make it taste even better?"

"Why should I listen to *you* about cooking tips?" he said roughly.

I turned to look at him and said, "My uncle is a chef."

"Oh," he responded. "Go on then, give us some of your uncle's chef tips."

"Well," I began. "If you're cooking with chicken then you must add some leeks. Chicken and leek stew tastes as though you are having your heart

hugged. Would you like your heart to be hugged?"

"A s*tew* can't hug your heart!"

"Oh yes it can, if it has enough leeks and plenty of cream."

The mole scratched his chin with his claw. "Hmm, I do like cream, and I do like hugs."

"And secondly, you probably know this already, but when you cook worm, you must add tarragon. You know about tarragon, don't you? It's a herb.

You do have some for the stew, don't you?"

The mole looked at the squirrel, and the squirrel looked at the crow. The crow shook his head.

"No, we don't," said the mole.

"Oh," I said, shaking my head, pretending to be sad that they didn't have any tarragon.

"What?" asked the mole.

"Well, if you add worm without the tarragon it's going to ruin the flavour of the whole stew. And if it ruins the flavour of the stew then you won't get that hug in your heart."

"But I WANT my HUG," said the mole, standing up.

The squirrel and the crow nodded their heads in agreement. "We just won't have the worm, then." He sat down again and folded his arms.

My plan was working. I was just about to offer to go and dig up some leeks when Laurence opened his great big beak.

"EXCUSE ME, EVERYBODY!" he said. "But I'm NOT actually a chicken. I'm a FLAMINGO, thank you very much. I shouldn't be in this stew, either.

We all know that flamingo doesn't go with leek."

"You're *not* a flamingo. Don't tell me lies.
I hate lies," said the mole, catching on to what
was happening.

"I'm not lying. I never *have* been and never *will*
be a chicken."

"You *are* a chicken!" The mole
shook his head. "You two rascals
are doing my head in."

"Who, ME as well?" I asked
innocently.

"Yes, especially you, you cheeky
worm, trying to trick me so that
I won't put you in the stew. I almost
believed you when you said that you have
an uncle who is a chef!"

I couldn't look at the
mole. He was right. My
uncle isn't really a chef;
he's a waiter.

"Right," the mole growled. "We're going back to the original plan. We're going to have CHICKEN and WORM soup."

He composed himself and carried on talking in a SMOOTH voice, "We'll wait for the water to get a little hotter. And then you two will have a *lovely hot bath*." The squirrel dropped some fresh vegetables into the pot. "You'll like that, won't you?"

"YES," we both said, going along with the mole's strange game of pretending that he was nice.

"I really like a hot bath with onions, carrots and potatoes," Laurence added.

We were back in the same terrible and hopeless situation. What made things worse was that Mole was sitting awfully close to me, so close that I could smell his breath through my worm skin.

It smelt like he'd eaten a whole raw onion, as if it were an apple. As each minute passed the smell became more and more unbearable. I had to do something to get away from the stench.

"While we're waiting for the water to boil, let's all have a dance!" I suggested.

"That's a great idea," said Laurence, standing up and wiggling his hips awkwardly.

"SIT down," said the mole. "There's no music, you feathered imbecile."

Laurence sat down and looked at the floor.

"Such a ridiculous idea," said the mole, looking at me. "How do you expect us to dance without any music playing?"

"We can make our own music," I said. Mole was about to start complaining again but I talked over him. "Squirrel, you can lay a beat for me, can't you? I need an eight beat."

The squirrel shot a glance at the crow. She was confused.

"What are you DOING?" whispered Laurence, loudly enough for everyone to hear.

"It's called beatboxing. It's like this." I pursed and flapped my mouth to make drumbeat sounds. As I did it, I had to take in deep breaths of onion air. I could now taste the onion as well as smell it.

"Can anyone do that for me? Laurence?"

Laurence started trembling.

I made the sounds again and wriggled my body to the beat, ignoring the onion smell. No one responded at first, but I continued.

 pbt ts pbts

After a while, the crow began to nod his head to the rhythm. The squirrel tried to make the same sound as me, but her teeth made it hard to make the **pbt** sound and it came out as a **ts ts ts**.

"That sounds like a snare drum," I said, trying to encourage her. I was quite good at being a beatboxing teacher. The squirrel smiled, showing her awful teeth.

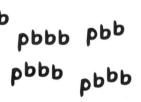

pbb
pbbb **pbb**
pbbb **pbbb**

"Let me have a go," said the mole, standing up.

It sounded like he was blowing a RASPBERRY.

74

"That, Mole," I said, "sounds a *lot* like a bass drum. Give us a **pbbb** on the first and second beats. See if you can do it from over there," I said, pointing to the opposite side of the shack, so that we would all have a break from his onion breath.

The crow joined in and gave a caw on the third and seventh beat.

"OK, so we'll all come in now on a five, six, seven, eight." Everyone was making a **pbt** or a **ts** or a **pbbb** noise, and we were all moving to the rhythm.

"Now it's time for us to do some dancing."

If I managed to get everyone dancing, then I might just be able to escape unnoticed.

"This move is called The Worm." I threw myself down to the ground and raised and dropped my body across the floor. "Can anyone else do that?"

The mole, squirrel and crow had fully immersed themselves in the music. They were tapping their feet and clapping their claws, paws and wings.

"I'm going to dance!" said the crow, waving his wings enthusiastically.

My plan was working. Laurence stood up to get a better view. The crow hopped towards us, and we all moved outwards to create a circle around  him. He paused momentarily and then began hopping and shuffling his feet to the rhythm.

"Great moves, Crow. Can anyone else do that?" I asked.

"Let me try," said the squirrel. She danced her way to the centre of the circle. The crow hopped backwards to make space for her. She wobbled around the circle with her elbows sticking out.

"My turn now," said the mole impatiently. He waddled to the middle and then swung his little arms from side to side while hopping from one foot to the other. He didn't have a very good sense of rhythm.

Everyone was mesmerized by the music, hopping and skipping about with their eyes closed. Everyone except for Laurence, who stood stiffly in the corner.

A goose and some ducks heard us and came into the hut. The dancing had become more ambitious. The squirrel leapt and did the splits in mid-air. The ducks were quacking, and the goose did a back flip that accidentally tore apart the whole shack.

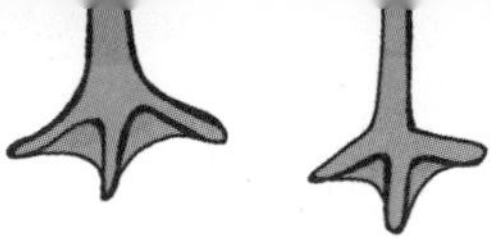

We were now standing in an open field.
I just needed to get Laurence dancing with
his eyes shut too, and then I'd be able to
properly escape from everyone.

"Laurence, can you do a tap dance?" I asked

as I did The Worm across
the floor.

"You saw before, I'm
not very good at dancing,"
he said, folding his
wings together.

"TAP-DANCE NOW!"
I said loudly, while staring
into his eyes.

Laurence
hopped swiftly to
the middle of the circle.
He tapped and shuffled his feet
with great precision at an incredible
speed. Everyone stopped what they were
doing to look at him.

He was an amazing tap-dancer. I felt proud
of him.

I couldn't dwell on that now, though. It was

my moment to run away. The soil was soft and perfect for digging. But as much as I wanted to be free, there was something stopping me.

It's true that Laurence had been an unlucky charm, but it felt funny now to leave without him. I'd sort of agreed to be his friend, and maybe being friends with him was a good idea. I started to make a list in my mind of the pros and cons of being friends with Laurence. I'd got as far as "he's really good at flying", which was on my list of pros, when I realized that the dance area was full of worms!

They had burrowed their way up from underground. They must have mistaken Laurence's tip tappity footsteps for the sound of rain. In worm society, when it rains, we all rise to the surface. It's just something that we do.

Laurence had no room to dance. Mole was agitated. And I'd missed my moment to run away.

"STOP THE BEATBOXING MUSIC!" Mole shouted, waving his claws about.

Everyone stopped their **pbbtting** and looked at him.

The dance party was over, and Mole was very, very angry.

Chapter Six

"Stop the dancing, STOP THE MUSIC!" Mole said again, waving his claws in big circles in the air. "Something is going on here, and I don't like it." He looked at all of us.

"Which one of you wigglers is Marcus?"

"*I* am Marcus," said a worm who wasn't me.

"Right, GET HIM," said the mole. "Throw him in the pot. The water must have boiled by now." The squirrel and the crow pushed their way through the throng of worms.

"*I* am Marcus," said another worm who wasn't me either, and was standing on the opposite side of the crowd. The squirrel and the crow looked at the mole to see what to do next.

The mole was standing on tip-toe to see whose voice it was.

"You can't *both* be Marcus!" he said angrily. "Which one of you is the *real* Marcus?"

One of the pretend Marcuses gave me a friendly wink when the mole wasn't looking. I giggled and looked at Laurence to see if he was finding this funny too.

Laurence's eyes were bulging out of his head again. He looked really confused.

Another worm spoke up. "I am Marcus."

And then another! And then *all* the worms pretended to be me, one by one.

"Right, that's it," said the mole. "Put them ALL in the stew pot!"

Everyone started screaming.

The crow hopped into the crowd and
tried to scoop everyone up with his wings.
The worms wriggled, wiggled and burrowed
quickly into the earth. The goose and the ducks
flew away, quacking and honking. There were
wings and feathers everywhere.

Through the commotion I could see
Laurence picking up a worm in his beak.
He flew up into the sky.

The crow looked at me. I was the only
worm left.

Before he could reach me with his feathery grasp, I dived into the soil, burrowing as quickly as I could. I dug down into the earth deeper and deeper – further down than I'd ever been before. I only stopped digging when I was too exhausted to move another millimetre.

"It's very quiet down here," I said out loud, even though there was no one around to hear me. I'd forgotten how quiet it was underground. "It's a long way from home too."

I felt anxious. Without Laurence I didn't have anyone to talk to or any idea how to get back home. Even *with* Laurence I wasn't sure how I would get back. I was stuck here in France, all on my own, for ever.

I became angry.

How dare Laurence fly off with another worm? We were supposed to be in this together. Surely Laurence couldn't have mistaken that other worm for me? We looked nothing like each other. I'd known Laurence since yesterday. Did he think that all worms looked the same or something?! Or maybe he *didn't* mistake me for another worm. Maybe he thought he'd try his luck finding a better navigator. What kind of friend drops another friend like that?! How could he be so selfish?

I shouted the angriest sentence I could think of.

"YOU ROTTER!"

No one could hear my angry words. I was totally by myself. I'd become used to Laurence's company and him just being there. Even though he could be trouble, mostly he was easy and fun to be around. I missed him. I really, really missed him. And it wasn't just because he had those sandwiches tucked away in his feathers and I was hungry.

Just then there was a muffled shuffling noise coming from above me.

"Gwenda?"

A head appeared in a freshly made hole from the ceiling of my mud chamber. It was one of the worms. She opened and closed her eyes. "Is that you?" she asked, looking at me with a big smile on her face.

She spoke excellent English. Everybody in France seemed to.

"*Non*, it's me," I said, making an effort to try to speak her language. "I'm the real Marcus."

"Oh," said the worm, her smile disappearing. She sighed heavily. "A fat bird who looked a bit like a chicken took Gwenda away. We heard you shouting and thought that you might have been her. We were hoping that he had dropped her and that she'd come back."

"It's only me, I'm afraid. I know that fat bird that you're talking about; he's Laurence. He wants to go to Lake Nakuru, and he probably expects Gwenda to navigate. You won't see *her* again," I said, snorting.

"We won't see Gwenda again?" the worm repeated, slowly. "We love Gwenda."

I felt guilty for being so flippant.

"Where is this Lake Nakuru?" she asked. "We'll have to go there so that we can bring her back home."

I couldn't bring myself to tell her where Lake Nakuru was. The only way they'd be able to get there was by making friends with some other birds who wanted to travel with worms and not be tempted to eat them for breakfast. That wasn't very likely.

"Where is Lake Nakuru?" the worm asked again with a worried voice.

"It's in Kenya, in Africa," I whispered softly.

"Africa! But that's miles away. She's not going to know the way to Africa."

I couldn't think of anything to say. We were both silent for ages. I started thinking about Robert the Bruce. We'd learnt about him in history at worm school. I don't remember most of the story, but the best bit was when everything was going wrong for Robert and he had to live in a cave to get away from the baddies. He was so bored that he ended up watching a spider trying to make a web. The spider kept falling down, but each time it would climb up and try again. Eventually after having loads of goes, the spider finished its web. This little spider inspired Robert the Bruce to never give up. I think he went on to do something important, but I can't remember that bit of the story, I just remember the spider part.

"Robert the Bruce once said, 'If at first you don't succeed, try, try again.'" I said to my dangling worm friend. I wasn't sure why I said that to her, but it must have been just what she needed to hear.

She looked at me with a sense of determination and said,

Sometime later, I stood with her among a circle of worms in a field. We were wearing stylish hats that had been decorated with twigs and dangly bits. One of the worms was arranging sticks in the middle of the circle. "This will help us get Gwenda back," he explained in a serious voice.

I looked at the sticks on the floor.

"Without further ado, let the ceremony BEGIN!" he announced.

All of the worms started wriggling in a circle around the twigs. I didn't have time to think about what I was doing, I just joined in. We were all chanting, "Come back, Gwenda. Come back, Gwenda. Come back, Gwenda."

As we went around and around in circles,
I wondered if I would be wearing a twig hat on
my head while chanting if I were back at home.
I thought to myself that I would have laughed
at this lot and said that they were all off their
rockers. But here in France I didn't have much
choice but to try to blend in with the locals, even
if they happened to be total weirdos.

I don't know how long we'd been chanting
for. It might have been thirty seconds, or it
could have been three hours, but I came out
of my trance-like state when a worm wearing

a fashionably dainty hat tilted
her head back and said loudly,
"HERE SHE COMES."

We all looked up.

A plump worm was falling
from the sky. We watched
as the worm grew bigger
and bigger as she got

closer and closer until she finally *whumped* on the ground before us.

"It's Gwenda," said one of the older worms.

I couldn't believe it! I'd never seen anything like it.

No one else seemed surprised. Everyone gathered around her.

"Now we will give thanks," a big worm said.

We began circling again. This time we had to chant, "Thank you, thank you, thank you."

Gwenda opened her eyes and sat up. She was shaking. We all wriggled in closer.

"Are you all right, Gwenda?" asked a worm with so many twigs on her hat that you could barely see her eyes.

"Yes," said Gwenda. "A scary chicken bird thing picked me up in his beak. I thought that he was going to eat me. He flipped me up in the air and I landed on his back. I was terrified.

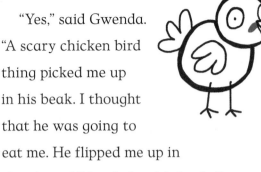

me

He was chatting away to me as if we were old friends, saying all sorts of rubbish. He was going on about how he didn't want the crow to put me in the stew pot and that he was sorry for being selfish about going to Africa. He said he was going to help me get back home to my worm life of digging holes in the mud. I thought to myself, *If you were that worried about me, why did you take me away in the first place?!*"

Listening to Gwenda speak,
I realized that Laurence thought
that she was me and he was
being kind in offering to take me home. I wanted
to take back all of the horrible thoughts that
I'd had about him. I wished that I hadn't called
him a rotter. I suddenly really liked Laurence

again and wished that he were here.
He was kind. I wanted to try to be
like him. *If he were here*, I thought to
myself, *I wouldn't let him take me home,
I'd properly navigate us to Lake Nakuru. That's
where he really wanted to be after all.*

Gwenda was still talking. "And then he was
saying, 'Marcus, Marcus,
can you hear me? Marcus,
have you fainted?'
And then I said,
'I'm not Marcus,
I'm *Gwenda*.'"

"That's when I lost my balance and fell out of the sky. I saw your pile of 'Come back Gwenda' twigs and somehow managed to fly towards them. That was probably the best part of this terrifying experience, and I'll be honest with you, I wouldn't mind doing that bit again.

"As I was falling, he was still going on! He apologized first for stealing and then dropping me. He said that if I see Marcus, I should tell him that Laurence is looking for him."

Everyone looked at me.

100

"YOU'VE GOT TO FIND LAURENCE!"
they said in one voice.

I sighed. "How can I find him? Look
up at the sky, it's massive. The world
is big, and I'm just a small and lowly
worm. There's no point in even
trying." I sighed again, a much
bigger one this time.

"I've got one word to say to you,"
said my underground, upside-down
dangling worm friend. "Robert the Bruce."

I didn't want to correct her by saying that
that was three words. I knew what she meant.
I couldn't give up.

"You're not on your own in this big world.
You've got us, and we will help you."

I was really glad to have met these French
worms.

They were kind and helpful.

I liked them, even though they were weirdos.

Chapter Seven

I was at the top of an unusual tower.

My French worm friends had come up with a plan to help Laurence find me. I would not be doing something as strange as this if I were back at home, but there was something about this lot and their firm belief that anything was possible that made me believe that this was going to work.

One of the worms had placed a crown of twigs on my head. I wondered if Laurence would like my fancy new hat.

Just as I was thinking that
thought, I heard a loud *swoosh* and
I was suddenly swept up into the
air in a bird's beak. I used all my
strength to twist round and see who
it was. It was Laurence!

Hanging
upside down,
my twiggy crown
fell from my head.
The twigs detached
themselves from the hat,
and one by one they tumbled
and landed on the ground.

It was a perfect way to say goodbye to my
lovely and unusual friends.

The worms hopped and beamed big smiles
up at me.

Laurence glided and landed in a nearby field. He was out of breath and his feathers were ruffled.

"I've been looking everywhere for you," he wheezed. "Are you all right?"

"Yes! Thank you very, very much for coming to get me."

"I took the wrong worm by accident, and then I was worried that the crow might have thrown you into the pot."

Laurence took a cheese sandwich from his feathers. He was leaning against a log, trying to get his breath back while eating his sandwich at the same time.

"Would you like to share this?" he asked.

"Yes, please," I said.

We ate in silence.

The sandwich had pickled onion in it. I love pickled onions.

"I really ought to take you back home," said Laurence, standing up. "I'm sorry for making you map-read and be the navigator for me. I don't exactly know the way back, but I'll make sure that you get safely home. It's the sensible and right thing to do."

"No," I said, squinting as I looked at Laurence. He was standing in front of the sun. "I want to do something for you. You've been such a good egg to me. I've thought about it, and I know how much it means to you to travel to Lake Nakuru and be with the flamingos. I'd like us to continue travelling there, together."

107

"No," said Laurence. "I really need to take you home. It would be very silly of us to continue with our journey when neither of us know the way. I've caused you too much trouble already."

I couldn't believe it. Laurence was thwarting my attempts to be kind. How dare he try to stop me from being nice? Did he not realize how difficult this was for me? It was really rude of him to say no when I was offering something as big as this. I wasn't going to let him stop me.

I INSIST that we go to Africa.

"Oh," said Laurence. He looked at his stomach. "I can't believe that you're saying this. I don't know what to say. Do you really think that we will be able to find our way to Lake Nakuru? Is that even possible?"

I hadn't actually thought about whether it was possible.

I started panicking. I was so desperate to try to be kind that I'd forgotten that I didn't actually know the way. Getting to Paris was just a fluke. There was no way that we'd ever find Lake Nakuru. Of course it wasn't possible. This whole trip had been one disaster after another.

I was just about to suggest that we *do* do the sensible and correct thing and go back home when Laurence said, "I accept your kind offer of travelling with me to Lake Nakuru. We didn't know the way to France, but together, we made it.

Marcus, you *are* an amazingly kind friend. I'm so glad that I met you. It might just be the best thing that's ever happened to me." He gave me a warm smile. I tried to smile back at Laurence, but it took a LOT of effort. It felt as though my face was covered in mud that had been baked by the sun.

Laurence didn't seem to notice; he was hopping around with excitement. "We'll go to bed now, and we'll get up very early to fly to Africa," he said, while bouncing in the air.

"Hooray!" I said in a monotone voice with my baked-mud smile. I was too exhausted to think about what to do next. My worm brain had been through too much in one day.

Laurence lay down on the long grass, ready to sleep. He offered me his feathery armpit to nestle my weary head.

I took him up on his offer, and he covered us both with the itchy blanket. Although the sun was still high in the sky, as it was only early afternoon, and although I had loads of fresh problems for my brain to solve, I fell into a deep and heavy, uninterrupted sleep.

Chapter Eight

When I woke up early the next morning, it was still dark. Laurence was talking to himself and hopping about, getting his things together. I remembered that I'd agreed to navigate our way to Lake Nakuru. I wanted to go back to sleep and pretend that this day wasn't happening.

"Do you think that it *is* the morning yet?" I asked. "Because apart from the moon, which is big and bright, the sky is as black as burnt sausages and all of the other birds are still asleep. I can hear them snoring."

"It *must* be the morning," he said. "We slept for ages and ages. Are you trying to have a sneaky lie-in, Marcus?"

"Heh heh, no!" I said, lying.

Laurence yawned and lowered his head for me to crawl up on to the back of his neck. Reluctantly, I climbed on.

He flew up into the burnt-sausage sky. The darkness made it easier for me to see; it was like being underground.
The air was
cool on my
worm skin.

Maybe, I thought to myself, *I could pretend that I was navigating to Africa, but instead I'd just lead us back home and then act surprised when we got there. That should be doable. It didn't take us that long to get to Paris. I'm sure that I would remember the way back if I saw a few familiar landmarks.*

I scanned the darkened countryside, looking for things that I recognized. I could see a big tree. I definitely remembered flying over a tree on the way here. "FLY TO THAT TREE ON YOUR LEFT, LAURENCE," I shouted out.

Immediately after the tree there was a field with a horse sleeping in it. I was a hundred per cent sure that I'd seen a horse on the way here. "Keep flying straight ahead, over the field."

We flew for a bit, then Laurence started to drop quite unexpectedly. "Are we landing?" I asked.

"No—er, no," he answered. He must have been a bit sleepy, like me.

This was going to be so easy. I could probably navigate with my eyes closed. I closed my eyes and yawned loudly.

"Are you still sleepy?" asked Laurence.

"Yes," I said. "Are you?"

"A little bit."

"I'm going to have a nap," I said, forgetting that I was supposed to be awake.

"That's a good idea. Night night," said Laurence.

I should have known that something was up. One minute I was flying with Laurence in the burnt-sausage sky, and the next moment we were both lying on some dusty, red soil in the heat of the sun. Laurence was sleeping and making whistling noises from his beak. A zebra was sniffing around his head.

"WAKE UP, LAURENCE!" I whispered loudly.

He opened his eyes and rubbed them with his wings. He saw the zebra, made a high-pitched scream, picked me up in his beak and flew up a tall tree.

The zebra looked up at us. She swished her black tail and then turned and nibbled on a piece of dry grass.

"That horse looks just like a zebra!" Laurence
squeaked.

"Yes, and that giraffe looks just like a giraffe!"
I said, pointing at a giraffe who was tearing at the
leaves on the branch that we were sitting on.

"Where are we?" Laurence gasped.

munch
munch

I looked around. There were four giraffes loitering around our tree. It was unlikely that we were back home. The only place that I'd seen these kinds of animals was in Laurence's Africa book. Maybe we *were* in Africa. Maybe I had directed Laurence to Africa in my sleep. That must be what happened! We'd actually made it to Africa!

A surge of excitement rushed through my worm body. Not because we were in Africa, but because I had discovered that I could sleep-navigate. What else could I do? Perhaps I was also a virtuoso-sleep-trumpet-player, or the world's greatest sleeping-brick-layer...

Laurence interrupted my daydreaming. "Marcus, I think that I flew us to Africa in my sleep! I can sleep-fly!"

"Really?" I asked, marvelling that we had both discovered sleeping talents at the same time.

"Yes, you told me to fly over a tree and then over a field. After that you didn't say anything for ages. When I was waiting for your next direction, I must have fallen asleep. I might have been flying for days, or weeks, or even years. And now look: this looks very much like the Maasai Mara National Park in Kenya! I can't believe that you knew the way, and that I flew us here."

"I can't believe it, either," I said to Laurence.

I had a feeling inside my body that I'd not experienced before. It was like a million happy butterflies that were fluttering their wings while singing a pleasant song. I wasn't even worried about how we would get home; I could probably sort that out while having an afternoon nap.

It was Laurence's dream to travel here, and together, without even trying, we'd actually done it … while dreaming!

Chapter Nine

"DO YOU SPEAK ENGLISH?" Laurence was shouting at the giraffe.

The giraffe looked at us with her very big eyes.

"COULD YOU GIVE US A RIDE?" he said slowly, this time doing a little mime.

The giraffe smiled and lowered her head so that we could climb on. She circled one of the tall trees, with Laurence and me balancing on her head.

Laurence turned to look at me. "This is brilliant, isn't it?"

It really was. I'd never
even dreamt of travelling,
but now here I was, balancing
on a giraffe's head in Kenya.
Beyond the trees, behind a
low fence, there were lots of
children with their mums and
dads. They were all pointing and
laughing and having fun.

The giraffe lowered her long neck to the ground, and Laurence and I hopped off.

"THANK YOU VERY MUCH," he shouted, doing a bow to show how grateful he was. "Are you all right, Marcus?" Laurence asked. "Your skin ... it looks a little *dry*."

I'd been enjoying myself on the giraffe so much that I hadn't noticed that my body was shrivelling in the dry heat of the sun. I tried to answer Laurence but couldn't move my mouth to speak.

"We'd better find some mud for you to cool down." Laurence picked me up in his beak and flew over some bushes and trees.

"There's a swamp!" he said, forgetting that I was in his beak and accidentally plopping me head first into the mud, which was cold and gloopy like thick, dark chocolate icing on a birthday cake. I sank to the bottom, and it felt utterly lovely.

I heard Laurence call to me with a muffled voice. "Everything OK down there?"

"Fine and dandy," I said, emerging from the swamp and feeling new again.

A big, pig-like creature watched me wriggle out of my muddy bath.

PLOP

"Hello, piggy," I said, trying to be friendly just in case he thought I was a chocolate-coated snack.

He snorted in my direction, giving me a shower that washed away the mud.

"Thanks, piggy," I said, keeping the conversation going just in case he thought I was now some kind of savoury snack.

"That's not a pig, it's a pygmy hippo," said
Laurence, who was reading a sign. "I must say,
it's very organized here in the Maasai Mara with
these informative signs."

There were signposts everywhere. And there were also neat paths edged with little fences. It did look quite different from Laurence's Africa books.

Laurence must have been thinking the same thing.

"It's not how I imagined it would be here," he said, hopping along a path. "I do like it; it's very tidy. In my safari books there were a lot more open spaces and dusty plains. It seemed more *natural*."

"I said it before, and I'll say it again, Laurence. That's progress for you."

Laurence nodded. "That must be what it is."

I remembered that I was brilliant at navigating, and I had the butterflies-in-my-tummy feeling again. "LAURENCE," I said, a little too enthusiastically.

"Yes?"

"Let's go and find that Lake Nakuru. It can't be far from here."

Laurence gasped.

"We can meet the flamingos," I said.

His eyes lit up. I wondered whether I needed to be asleep to find the way or whether I might be able to find it just by using my worm instincts.

"Maybe one of these signposts will direct us to the lake," Laurence said, hopping speedily along the path. "Ooh, there's a map here as well," he called out. "Can you come and look at it?"

Silly Laurence, he had obviously forgotten that I don't need a map to navigate.

"*Psst*," said the pygmy hippo. "If you're looking for the flamingos, they live in the middle of the lake on the other side of the giraffes' house." He lifted his head to point out the direction to go.

"Thank you very much," I said. Even though he'd told me the way, I probably could have worked it out with my natural worm instincts.

The hippo gave me another spray of water.

It lifted me along the path like a water slide. This water spraying thing was probably a local custom. I filled my cheeks with water from a puddle and sprayed him back.

It didn't have quite the same impact, but hopefully he appreciated the gesture.

I rejoined Laurence, who looked as though he was using all of his bird brain to try to understand the map.

"Come on," I said. "*I'm* the navigator."

I jumped up onto his back without waiting for him to lower his neck. I missed and slid down the side of his wing. Laurence picked me up with his beak and threw me onto my usual seat.

We flew up past the tall building, over some lions and a group of penguins.

In geography class at worm school they taught us that penguins lived in cold countries. Why were there penguins here in Africa? Maybe they were on a special tour. That was probably it.

"Oh, look, there are kangaroos over there," said Laurence as we flew over a big hill. "I didn't expect to see kangaroos here. I thought they just lived in Australia."

"They're on holiday," I said confidently. "They're on the same tour as the penguins."

"Oh, I see," Laurence answered. Just then I could see something glistening in the distance.

"Laurence! There it is... It's over there. I can see it! I can see it! We've made it! It's Lake Nakuru!"

We landed at the edge of the lake next to some tall trees. To celebrate this moment, Laurence was singing a song. I *think* it was a song: I didn't recognize the tune or the words but he looked as though he was enjoying the strange noises that were coming from his beak.

I was about to do a happy
dance when from the corner of my eye
I saw a squirrel. It was a familiar-looking
squirrel. It looked just like the one with
the awful teeth who was friends with
the evil mole.

I had a funny feeling in my belly.

Chapter Ten

"What are you looking at?" Laurence asked.

The squirrel had darted away, and I was staring at an empty branch.

"Do you remember that squirrel from before?"

"Ooh, yes," said Laurence, doing a weird body shake. "That was when we were almost a stew!"

"I think that I just saw her, Laurence."

"Why would she be here in Africa?" Laurence asked. "You must have imagined it."

"Yes," I said, laughing. I laughed even though it wasn't funny.

I looked up at the tree again, to double-check. No squirrels. It must have been my silly imagination.

I turned back to Laurence. He was staring straight ahead with his beak open. He looked as though he'd just seen something spectacular, like a unicorn or a pile of chips with cheese on top.

"What is it?" I asked, looking to see if there was a unicorn, or cheesy chips.

"It's them! My flamingo family!" he said with a soft, crackly voice.

Laurence was looking at a small group of pink birds with long, thin legs who were standing on an island in the middle of the lake. A tear was rolling down his cheek.

They really *were* flamingos. We stood in silence, watching from a distance. We stared at them for so long that I started to wonder if the flamingos were actually real. They were bright pink with unusual beaks and legs that looked like twigs. Maybe they *were* made out of plastic and twigs?

Then one of the flamingos gracefully bent down, scooped a fish out of the water and gulped it down.

"I think they *are* real," I said out loud.

Laurence sighed. "This is where I belong. It's my true home. I can't believe that we actually made it here," he said, staring ahead.

I couldn't believe it either. I looked at Laurence and then at the flamingos and then at Laurence again. He still looked like a chicken – a little, fat, round one. I thought about telling him. Maybe he hadn't noticed. But then I remembered about trying to be kind and that in Laurence's mind he *was* a flamingo. It was probably best to try to support Laurence in whatever he believes. That's probably what a friend would do.

"I've always dreamt of meeting flamingos, and now it's finally happening," Laurence went on. "I'm *one* of them."

"Yes, you are," I said, lying to Laurence.

"Shall we go and meet them?" Laurence asked.

"Yes," I said.

We flew to the island in the lake and landed next to a small group of flamingos. I couldn't help staring at their legs. Up close they looked even more like twigs. Laurence must have been having a good look as well because one of the flamingos said to him, rudely, "What are you staring at, little bird?"

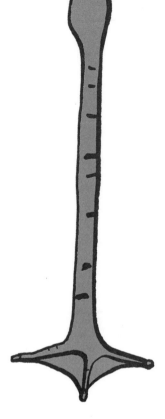

"All of you," he said boldly, pushing his chest out. I think he was trying to make himself look a bit taller. "My companion and I," Laurence said in a posh voice, "have travelled many, *many* miles from a distant land to meet all of you."

He extended his wing to
include me in the conversation.
He sounded and looked a bit like
the Queen of England.

I cleared my throat and sat up straight, to appear more regal.

He continued, "All of my life I've dreamt of meeting flamingos and finding true friendship, happiness and a sense of belonging. Now that time has come. As you can probably tell, *I* am a flamingo, and it is my honour to be reunited with all of you, my brothers and my sisters."

Laurence's speech was actually quite good.

The flamingos didn't say anything at first. They looked at us with their beaks open. I had a feeling that they might not be very friendly. I was right because then something horrible happened:

a small flamingo with a scratchy voice started laughing. It wasn't the type of nice laughing that you get when children are running around on a beach, splashing in the waves. No, it was a cruel, mocking sound. It made my skin hurt. All of the other flamingos joined in.

I wanted for Laurence and me to be somewhere else, far away from these horrible birds. I imagined us being in Paris on a bicycle made for two with *two* freshly baked baguettes in the front basket. This made me happy, being somewhere else.

And then I remembered again that I can't ride a bicycle. I felt sad.

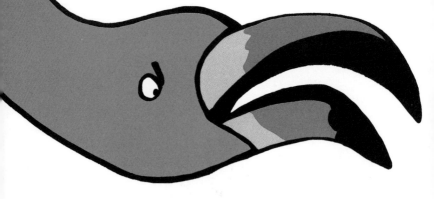

Normally in a situation like this I would have found an excuse to wriggle away, but because I was with Laurence and he was standing there like a bronze statue with its beak wide open in shock, I had to stand there as well, to try to be supportive.

The first flamingo lowered his head to Laurence's level and whispered, "You're not one of *us*. You're just a common, plain bird. *No one* is interested in your type."

He and his friends turned their backs to us and walked away on their twigs. I couldn't believe how rude he was. I felt *really* angry. I wanted to do something that would make a difference. I powered up my worm brain to think of something that would help Laurence.

"Shall I go and hit him?" I asked.

"No, don't do that," Laurence said.

I was glad because I'd not hit anyone before. That was another thing that they didn't teach us in worm school.

As I stood there, feeling like a tiny, helpless worm, I remembered Robert the Bruce. Well, not *Robert*, but the spider who inspired him to never give up. If that spider were here now, he'd probably tell me to go and stand up for Laurence.

With that in mind, I wriggled over to the group of flamingos and said in my boldest voice, "And WHAT do you THINK you are DOING?" The flamingos turned to look at me.

try

They looked confused. "I said, WHAT DO YOU THINK YOU ARE DOING?"

The flamingos looked at the ground with sullen faces, suddenly ashamed. I couldn't believe that they were listening to me! I felt as big as a tall building.

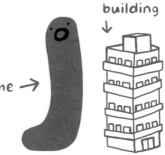

building

me →

"We're not doing nothing," mumbled the one with the scratchy voice.

"You're not doing ANYTHING," I said, correcting his grammar while wriggling slowly and deliberately in a circle around the four of them.

"What's he doing?" asked a flamingo with a big beak, who was now looking quite worried.

"I heard the way that you spoke to this bird, Laurence." Laurence flew and stood by my side.

"YOU flamingos have been very RUDE and DISRESPECTFUL to him."

One of the flamingos looked up for a moment, her face full of indignation.

"I want you to apologize," I said.

The birds crossed their wings and huffed and muttered under their breaths. "I'm not going to apologize," one of them mumbled.

"NOW!" I said, pretending that I was as big as a skyscraper.

"Sorry, Laurence," they said in unison.

That was good, I thought to myself. I liked being a skyscraper. "And WHY are you sorry?"

"For being rude and disrespectful," they all said together.

"That's right."

"Can we go now?" asked the flamingo with a big beak.

"No, I want you to say to Laurence, '*You* are a flamingo. You are the *best* flamingo of us all.'"

There was silence.

"But he's not actually a flamingo," said the smaller flamingo cautiously.

"I DON'T CARE if he's a flamingo or not. I just want you to SAY it and make my friend HAPPY."

Laurence cleared his throat and put his wing in the air.

"Yes, Laurence?"

"I think, maybe," he said softly, "I'm not a flamingo." His voice went up at the end as if he was asking a question even though he wasn't.

"I *may* have made a mistake. I *thought* I was a flamingo, but now that I'm here and *they're* here I can see that we look just a little bit different. I think that maybe we're different types of bird." He was whispering so quietly that all of us had to lean in to hear what he was saying.

"Do you still want us to say that he's a flamingo?" asked the flamingo with the scratchy voice.

"NO. YOU MAY BE DISMISSED," I said loudly.

"Thank you very much," they replied and turned around.

"Goodbye, and remember..." I said without finishing my sentence.

They stopped and turned their heads.

I made them wait a while before continuing.

"...be good."

They all nodded and continued on their way, wading through the lake.

Laurence picked me up, and we flew to a bench by some tall trees.

"What was that all about?" he asked, in a high-pitched giggling voice.

"What?" I asked, feeling my worm-like self returning.

"You were like a different worm. I've not seen you act like that before."

"I was inspired by a spider, and I pretended that I was as big as a tall building."

"Oh," said Laurence, who seemed to understand but then looked as though he really didn't know what I was talking about. "Whatever it was," he said, "thanks for sticking up for me. You're really kind." He put his wing on my back to show his appreciation.

I felt another feeling that I'd not felt before. It was as if someone had opened a bottle of lemonade inside my head. My face felt fizzy.

"Are you embarrassed?" Laurence asked. "Your cheeks have gone a funny colour."

"I prefer gherkins to pickled onions because they look like dinosaur toes," I said, trying to change the subject. "I don't like mustard, though, it tastes like fire." It was overwhelming having so many feelings all at once.

"What are you talking about?"

"I don't like mustard," I said.

"Oh. But mustard is really nice, how can you not like it?" asked Laurence, taking his wing away from my back.

"Mustard is the worst! It's like eating a..." I stopped mid-sentence. From the corner of my eye I could see that squirrel again. It *was* her, the one with the horrible teeth.

And she was beatboxing.

Chapter Eleven

"What is *she* doing here in Lake Nakuru?" asked Laurence. He'd taken another sandwich from his feathers and was eating and speaking with his beak full. He offered me half, but it had mustard in it, and, as I'd said before, I really don't like mustard.

"Maybe she's on holiday with the kangaroos."

We watched her beatboxing and dancing.

"I taught her how to do that," I said. "She must have practised because she's much better than she was before."

The squirrel was doing cartwheels in a circle and full backward body spins in the air. The humans loved it. They were laughing and making kissy noises with their lips so that she would look at them. Every now and again she would stop dancing and scamper over to a person, and they would give her a peanut.

"I've had another thought," I said with dread. "Maybe they're following us – her, the mole and that crow. And they're going to put us in the cooking pot after all."

"I think she is just on holiday," said Laurence firmly. "She looks too relaxed to be up to any mischief." Laurence looked over his shoulder, just in case.

The squirrel saw us. She stopped her acrobatic dance and beatboxing routine. Then she smiled a toothy grin while forward flipping over to us. I wondered if Laurence had packed any peanuts in his feathers.

"Quick," said Laurence. "Let's get out of here!"

"Marcus! Wait!" the squirrel called out. "I need to say something."

She'd remembered my name, and she almost sounded warm and friendly. This was confusing.

Laurence must have been confused too. He had me dangling from his beak and was standing in a take-off position, ready to fly away. He waited for her to say something else.

"I just wanted to thank both of you for teaching me how to dance," she said.

"OK," said Laurence, dropping me from his

beak onto the ground. I wished that he would remember that he can't speak and hold me in his beak at the same time.

"We can be friends, if you like. My name is Jennifer-Peggy – or J-Peg, for short."

"Umm," said Laurence nervously.

J-Peg continued. "Before meeting you, I was scrawny and hungry all of the time. Then you two came and taught me how to beatbox and dance; it meant that I could move *here*. Humans give me loads of peanuts to reward me for my routines. I haven't been hungry for ages thanks to you."

She did look much healthier now.

"Oh!" Laurence started patting his feathers down as if he were looking for something. "We don't seem to have any *peanuts* with us, but please take this," he said, offering her half of his cheese-and-mustard sandwich. "You must have been *SO* hungry to travel all this way just to get a few peanuts. You poor thing."

159

J-Peg looked confused, but she gratefully took the sandwich.

"Thank you very much. That's kind of you." She looked up at us with a remorseful expression on her face. "I'm sorry about what happened with the stew before, with the others. I didn't *really* want to eat you. I was just hungry."

"That's quite OK," said Laurence, quickly passing her the rest of the sandwich. "We wouldn't want you to go without any food."

J-Peg gave us a big smile, and, even though she had awful teeth, she looked beautiful.

She put the sandwiches in her mouth and scuttled up a big tree. When she got to the top branch, she waved at us.

Laurence waved back to her.

"I didn't expect to see *her* here," he said. I nodded in agreement.

"And won't you look at that!" said Laurence, putting his wing around my shoulder. "I can see my neighbours from home over there, eating ice cream." He waved at them as well, and they waved back. "Marcus, it's like we're living in a film that is full of funny coincidences. This is such a brilliant film."

Something didn't quite feel right. So far we'd seen J-Peg, the kangaroo, some penguins and there in front of us were Laurence's neighbours. They couldn't all be on a holiday tour. And another funny thing was that no matter where we were in the world, everyone spoke with a perfect English accent. In worm school they taught us languages so that we could speak to worms from other countries. It took me ages to learn Mandarin.

"Laurence, do you think that perhaps we might not be in Lake Nakuru after all?"

"Of course we are!" Laurence answered hastily. He took his wing away from my shoulder. "Whatever in the world makes you think that we're anywhere *but* Lake Nakuru?"

"Hello, Laurence," said one of Laurence's neighbours. He had hopped over to join us.

"Bernard! Hello!" said Laurence, who was beginning to sweat now.

"Would you like some of my ice cream?" Bernard asked.

"No, thank you. Are you on holiday, Bernard?"

"No," he said, taking a lick from his ice cream.

"Oh," said Laurence. He looked around.

"Bernard?"

"Yes?"

"We are in Lake Nakuru, aren't we?"

"No, Laurence. We're at the zoo," said Bernard casually.

"The *zoo*? Oh. Is it a zoo in Lake Nakuru?"

"No," said Bernard. "It's a zoo that's ten minutes from where we live."

"Really?" said Laurence. He thought for a moment. "But it *can't* be, because we've been flying for days to get here and we even flew past the Eiffel Towers in Paris, which must mean that we're in Africa now. *And* we've seen lots of wild animals as well – the kind of animals that *only* live in Africa."

"I'm not sure why it took you days to get here, Laurence," Bernard said, taking another lick from his ice cream. "Maybe you came the long way round, through Paris. Or," he said, tipping his head to one side to think, "it could be that the Eiffel Towers that you saw were the pylons. They sort of look like the Eiffel Tower. Pylons are used to carry electricity, and there are lots of them near where we live. And as for the animals ... well ... you get all kinds of animals in a zoo."

"I thought we were in *Kenya*," said Laurence, looking as though he might cry.

"Well, maybe we are. I'll check," said Bernard. I think he was trying to make Laurence feel better.

"TANYA!" he shouted.

"Yes?" asked Tanya. She was eating a strawberry ice cream and there were blobs of it all around her beak.

"Are we in Kenya?"

"No, Bernard. We're at the zoo. Why?"

"Just checking," said Bernard. "Sorry about that, Laurence. We *are* at the zoo. Are you sure you don't want some of this ice cream?" He put the cone under Laurence's beak.

Laurence took the cone.

Instead of taking one lick – which was what Bernard was offering – he slowly ate the whole thing while staring into space.

Bernard watched Laurence with his beak open. "If you need to get home," he said, "just fly over these trees and keep going straight. You'll see the Eiffel Towers, and after two more fields you'll get to our tree."

"Thank you," said Laurence, looking at the ground.

"And another thing ... we come here all the time. You can come with us on the next visit, if you like."

"Thank you," said Laurence, still looking at the ground.

Bernard hopped back to the others. They were talking and looking over at us in between licks of their ice creams.

Except for Bernard, who didn't have an ice cream.

Chapter Twelve

Laurence and I were sitting on the ground.

I couldn't believe it. We had just been flying around in giant circles the whole time, going nowhere. I thought I knew how to navigate in

my sleep, and Laurence thought he had learnt
how to sleep-fly. There was a moment when both
of us felt on top of the world, where anything
was possible with our shared secret genius
skills. But it turned out that we were both still
as useless as when we had first met each other.
The whole experience had been a pointless waste
of time.

Laurence was probably really depressed
now. It was my job to try to think of something
helpful and supportive to say. I couldn't think
of anything.

"Have you got any sandwiches with pickle
left?" I asked.

Laurence rummaged in his feathers with his
wing, looking for extra sandwiches. "No. I gave
the last sandwich to that squirrel because
I thought that she'd walked all the way to
Lake Nakuru – for a peanut."

Without meaning to, I laughed.

Laurence looked at me. "It's not funny," he said.

Then *he* started laughing. I'm not sure why, but both of us couldn't stop laughing, and people stopped to look at us. Laurence wheezed and thumped the ground with his wing.

"We've just been flying in circles for DAYS!" he said. "And THEN when we got here and saw the flamingos, they were REALLY rude."

"They were SO rude," I said in between laughing fits. "I can't *believe* that you wanted to be a flamingo. No, I can't believe that you thought that you *were* a flamingo."

"But I *do* look like a flamingo," Laurence said.

I laughed so much at this that I thought that my stomach might explode.

"You don't look *anything* like a flamingo," I said. "You look like a chicken."

I was bent over double, but when I finally finished laughing I noticed that Laurence had stopped laughing ages ago.

"Do you think that I look like a chicken?" he asked seriously.

"No ... you don't, Laurence," I said, suddenly worried that I might have hurt his feelings. "Well, you do sort of look like a chicken."

Then I got annoyed.

"What's wrong with looking like a chicken? All of your neighbours look like chickens, and there's nothing wrong with them. I don't know why you want to be something different. You're brilliant just as you are."

"Am I?" he asked.

I'd just said something nice to Laurence without thinking about it in advance. Was Laurence really brilliant?

"Yes, you are brilliant, Laurence," I said.

"Oh," he said.

I wasn't used to having conversations like this. I waited for him to change the subject. But then, without thinking, loads of words came out of my mouth: "It doesn't matter that you look like a little round chicken. What matters is that you are kind. You could have eaten me for breakfast, but you didn't. You told me about your dream to fly to Lake Nakuru, and then you took me there, sort of. I was scared at first and only agreed to come because I didn't have any choice, but in the end it turned out to be much more fun than staying at home digging holes in the mud. I prefer being with you to digging holes in the mud, Laurence."

Laurence didn't say anything for a while. Then he said, "That's the nicest thing that anyone has ever said to me."

I felt a warm glow. I'd said something nice without trying or even lying.

Laurence looked at me and said, "I thought that I'd only be happy if I moved to Lake Nakuru in Kenya and made friends with flamingos. But these last few days I've been happier than I've ever been before. I'm not in Kenya, and I'm not a flamingo. But I didn't need to be a flamingo; I just needed a friend. And you're my friend. Thank you, friend."

"That's OK, friend," I said.

This conversation was getting too much for me. I had that lemonade-in-the-head feeling again. It was too embarrassing for us to look at each other, and I was beginning to feel dizzy and sick. We both stared straight ahead.

A pigeon was standing on a sandwich that had fallen on the floor. He pecked at it hurriedly before any of the other pigeons spotted it. It was an egg and cress sandwich.

"Do you want to come to my house for dinner later?" Laurence asked.

"What will you be making?" I asked.

I wondered what the pigeon would be having for dinner. Perhaps it would be another sandwich.

"Mashed potato."

Mashed potato is one of my favourites.

"Yes, please, Laurence," I said.

Chapter Thirteen

It didn't take us three days to fly back from "Lake Nakuru National Park" to Laurence's house, but it might have done if Tanya hadn't spotted us as we took off. We had been flying in the wrong direction.

Tanya ended up staying for dinner, and
Laurence invited his neighbours Lizzie,
Bernard and Shakira – and that pigeon.
His name was Sebastian.

Laurence wasn't used to having
dinner parties. He started panicking
in the kitchen, and then ended up
making too much mashed potato.

The extra potato was enough to make a mashed-potato bed. Laurence slept in it that night and said that it was the most comfortable bed in the world.

zzzzzzzzz

When I met Laurence for the first time, he had his beak wide open, ready to eat me. I didn't stop to wonder if he might be kind and thoughtful and have a penchant for cheese-and-mustard sandwiches. No, I just wanted to get as far away as I could from the beaky fluffball. I was quite content with my life, hidden under the ground digging worm tunnels in the dark.

And when Laurence met me, he didn't stop to wonder if I would be the sort of worm who would care about the things that he cared about. No, he just saw a tasty breakfast.

We were very lucky that we had a conversation about our hobbies. If it wasn't for that, then we wouldn't have discovered that we could do things together that were impossible on our own.

With Laurence, I can fly.

And if Laurence hadn't met me, he would probably still be at home, sitting on his sofa like a blob of mashed potato and thinking about his dreams, but not doing anything about them. All of his life he had dreamt about faraway places.

It was only when he met me and we left his birdhouse for Lake Nakuru that he became a courageous adventurer.

In the end we didn't make it to Lake Nakuru, or to France, or even further than three miles away from the birdhouse. But we *did* have an adventure. We discovered those pylons, and that was probably just as good as seeing the Eiffel Tower. We escaped from a cooking pot and rode a giraffe.

Laurence did a dance in front of everyone without worrying about what people thought about him. He even rescued a worm, Gwenda – who didn't really want to be rescued, but it was the thought that counted.

I chanted in a circle with weird worms while wearing a hat made of twigs on my head, and we both slept out under the burnt-sausage sky sharing an itchy blanket.

One of my favourite things about Laurence is that I can tell him the thoughts in my head and he doesn't say, "What a ridiculous idea!" or anything horrible like that.

The other day I told him about how I sometimes daydream about riding a bicycle with a freshly baked baguette in the front basket. He didn't say anything. I thought that he'd fallen asleep, but he hadn't because the very next day he came to my house with a big surprise.

He had an actual bicycle for me, with a basket
on the front! It wasn't even my birthday. I love it
so much.

I did try to ride it, but it's quite hard riding
a bicycle when you're a worm. So, to help me
out, Laurence rides it and I sit in the basket and
pretend to be the freshly baked baguette.

Sometimes J-Peg the squirrel comes to visit,
and *she* rides the bike and Laurence sits in the
basket and pretends to be the baguette.

Even though Laurence is a bird and I am a worm, he doesn't see me as breakfast any more. He sees me as his friend. I think that's why he doesn't seem to notice the things that I can't do well. He just sees the good things in me, things that even I don't always see. Maybe what he sees is the real me, the real Marcus. I don't know... But I do know that Laurence is probably the kindest living bird on the planet, and he makes me want to try to be a better worm.

It's hard for me to be as kind and nice as he is, and I keep doing it wrong, but then I remember Robert the Bruce and his unusual little friend who happened to be a spider. It reminds me that if at first I don't succeed, then try, try again.

Thanks

With special thanks to everyone at Walker Books.
Especially my wonderful editor Lizzie for pulling out
all of the stops to make this book happen, for her
infectious laughter, brilliantly funny ideas, dedication
and all round good egg-ness. Thanks to Linas who
also edited and is a joy and a hoot to work with.
To David and Jacky for patiently putting the words
and pictures together.

Thanks to Mirielle, Frances, Mickey, Alice, Jane
and Angel for big hearts, being open and laughing
in the right places. You all helped create the bird
that looks like a chicken.

And with extra massive thanks for the unwavering
love, care and support of Tim who has always
believed in me and that no matter what happens,
like Laurence and Marcus, together we can fly.

About the Author

Award-winning comic artist Simone Lia began painting and drawing in her dad's tool shed at the age of 13 before going on to study at the University of Brighton and then the Royal College of Art. She has written comic strips for children and adults for numerous publications including *The Observer* with "Things That I've Learnt", "The Chip and Bean Quiz" in *The Independent on Sunday* and "Sausage and Carrots" in *The DFC*. She has also published graphic novels *Fluffy* and *Please God, Find Me a Husband*. Her work has been exhibited across Europe, including the Tate Britain. Simone lives and works in London.

Look out for my new book, coming soon!